This book was very loved
But we needed room for new.
We hope you will enjoy it
Just as much as we did, too.

nhfpl
NEW HAVEN FREE PUBLIC LIBRARY

Fat... ...Blues

DATE DUE

For my Daddy Charles Hubert Smith
and "I Love you Black Child"
I.S.

To my close friends – the Hancocks, Owens,
Gradys, Buells, Kitty, Moe, the Coles, Cybels,
Phineas, Jane and Marfy.

K.M.

ISBN: 0-681-00543-2

1st Edition

0 9 8 7 6 5 4 3 2 1

Father's Day Blues

WHAT DO YOU DO ABOUT FATHER'S DAY WHEN ALL YOU HAVE ARE MOTHERS?

COMPOSITION BOOK

Name Cheryl Blues
School Garfield Elementary

LONGMEADOW
PRESS

BY IRENE SMALLS • ILLUSTRATED BY KEVIN McGOVERN

"Father's Day! Why all this fuss about Fathers? Granny, you do the cooking, Aunt Grace fixes things and Ma works. What do daddies do anyway?" Cheryl asked, leaning back in the kitchen chair.

"What kind of question is that?" Grandma asked with a laugh. She stepped back from her baking.

Cheryl twirled her hair with her finger. "I have to write a composition entitled "My Daddy" for Father's Day...I wanted to ask the teacher what to do if you don't have a daddy. Then, Yvonne, this girl in my class, skinned up her nose at me. Yvonne thinks she's better than me."

Cheryl pranced across the kitchen, mimicking Yvonne in a singsong voice. "'It's a shame the way some folks don't have a daddy.' Huh, just 'cause Yvonne's daddy comes home every night." Cheryl slumped. "I do have a Daddy. He just doesn't live with me. That's all."

Grandma, who laughed and cried with the ease of the sun bringing morning, said, "Menfolks are the same as womenfolks. See that baby boy toddling over there? That baby doesn't know whether he's a man-child or a girl-child. He just knows that he needs to be loved." She grabbed Aunt Grace's baby and gave him a kiss.

Little Larry, squirming free, toddled back to his toys.

Cheryl screwed up her face. She still wasn't satisfied.

Seeing her look, Grandma said, "Don't fret yourself. Sometimes grown folks get confused and they make mistakes. But that doesn't take anything away from how wonderful and special you are."

"Yeah, but things should be different," Cheryl said.

"Sometimes things are not always the way they should be," Grandma answered.

*A*unt Grace, a tall angular woman who made sharp corners where none existed, came into the room with a broken doll. Aunt Grace snapped, "Daddy talk! Your mother's your mother all the days of her life. Your father's your father till he gets a new wife."

"Your father's your father all the days of your life too," Grandma replied.

Cheryl's head bobbed between the two women.

*A*unt Grace, reaching for the glue in the cabinet drawer, snapped again. "A father works from sun to sun. A mother's work is never done."

"A father's work is never done either," Grandma said, flour flying.

Then, more gently, Grandma said to Cheryl, "Menfolks are just built a little different from womenfolks, that's all. Menfolks like to laugh just like womenfolks, menfolks cry just like womenfolks—though they won't let on—and menfolks try to do the best they can. Same as us."

Aunt Grace gave the repaired doll to Cheryl. Mad, Aunt Grace stomped off toward the living room.

"In this life sometimes you've got to overlook some folks," Grandma stated, looking at Aunt Grace strut off.

"Me and my husband had good times, bad times, and lots of laughs. When he died, I remembered the good times the most." Grandma chuckled, lovingly patting her dough. She rose and gave Cheryl a kiss.

Cheryl helped Grandma make supper.

After supper Cheryl went to her bedroom. She reached down in the bottom drawer and grabbed the package of her daddy's old clothes. She smelled them. The overalls had a musty odor. "That must be Daddy's smell," Cheryl said. Then she tried to talk in a gruff voice. Daddy sounds, she called it. She thought about what to write for her Father's Day paper, but thinking about her daddy made her sad and she was unable to write.

*L*ater that evening Cheryl squeezed her eyes and strained to remember her daddy, pretending he was with her. All she remembered was a pair of big hands holding her, patting her. She took out the old picture of her daddy that her mother kept in the bureau drawer. Cheryl saw a coffee-colored man with a smile that lit up the sky. She started to cry. Cheryl stared at her own face in the mirror.

$\mathcal{H}$er mother came in and asked, "What are you doing?"

"I'm trying to see if I'm missing anything," Cheryl whispered.

"Missing anything?"

"One of the teachers said that without a daddy you're missing something."

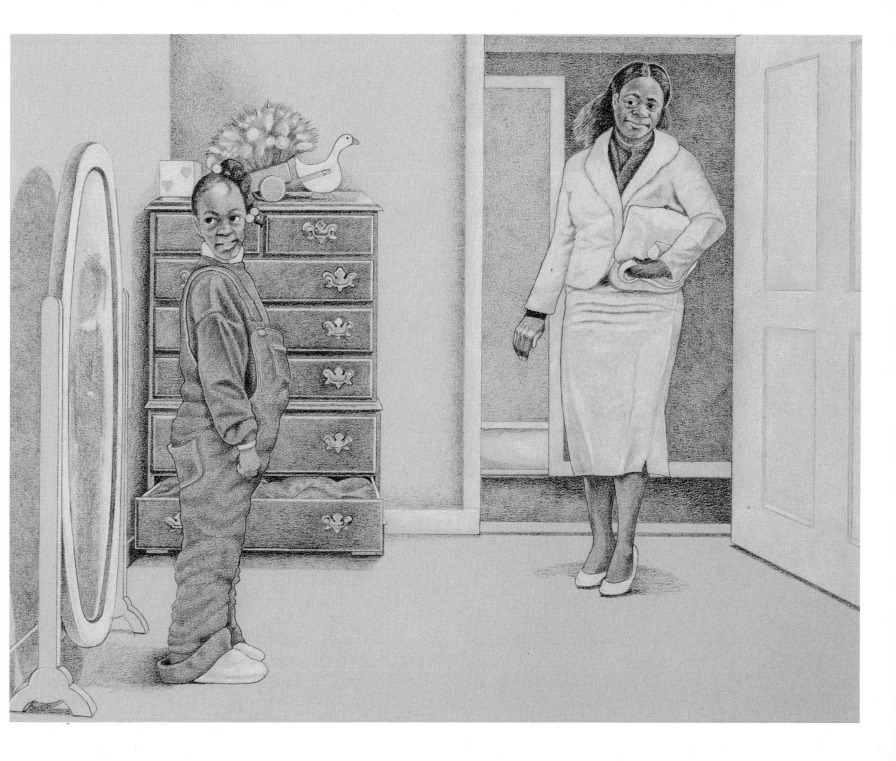

Cheryl's mother's eyes grew large and wet. "Your daddy's not being around isn't your fault," she said. "Think about the love you have. Grandma loves you, Aunt Grace loves you, and I love you."

Cheryl's mother hugged Cheryl in the puff of her shoulder. "You are the love of my life," she sang. "You are wonderful."

Cheryl thought for a while. Then she smiled. "I guess you're right," Cheryl answered. She got her paper and pencil again.

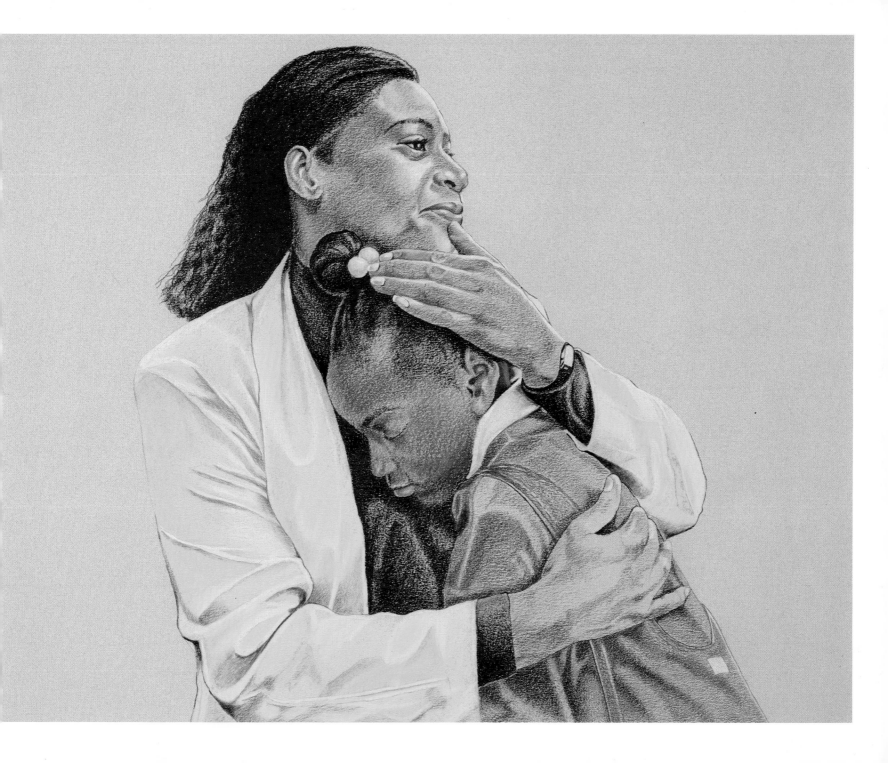

When Cheryl reached school the next day, the first person she saw was Yvonne.

"Did you do your composition?" Yvonne asked.

"Of course I did," Cheryl answered.

*M*iss Bennett, the teacher, asked for volunteers to read before the class. Cheryl hesitated. After hearing how Lee Chin had come from China with only his grandmother, Cheryl raised her hand.

Miss Bennett called on her, "Cheryl Blues." Cheryl rose stiffly, suddenly scared.

"My Daddy." Cheryl started with the title of the composition. "My daddy isn't living with us anymore, but I love him. Not having a daddy around isn't that bad. When you're little you think that everybody lives the same as you, and their daddy isn't around either. But now I know some children see their daddy every day and some kids see their daddies only once in a while. I know one thing. It's not the kid's fault whoever their family is made up of. Sometimes grown-ups' business is something kids don't understand. Grandma says, 'If you don't understand it, just keep on living.' Maybe when I'm older I'll understand why my daddy left. Right now, I don't. My name is Cheryl Blues and I'm not sad. I'm glad about me. The end."

"That was excellent, Cheryl," Miss Bennett said. "All our families are different, but love is what makes a family."

Cheryl sat down and didn't even look at Yvonne. She couldn't wait to tell Grandma, Ma, and Aunt Grace that her teacher had said Cheryl's composition was excellent. "Excellent." Cheryl repeated the word.

Cheryl hopped home. Hopping wasn't a daddy step. Daddies walked. But it was a Cheryl step. Cheryl was proud of herself and she knew her daddy would be proud of her too.